At **THE DAVID BECKHAM ACADEMY** every day is a footballing adventure. Boys and girls come along to learn about the sport, develop their skills and have fun. But it's not just about tricks and flicks . . . As David Beckham knows, the real secret behind being a Premier League player is understanding the importance of dedication, teamwork, passion and having belief in yourself. In these pages you can meet football-mad children and follow them as they live out their dreams at The Academy.

SO STEP INS
JOIN THE

Want to know what some of our readers thought of this book?

'This book made me laugh out loud!'

Chandrika, age 8

'Kids my age will really like this book'

Kieran, age 7

'I learnt about teamwork'

Emily-Mae, age 7

'I liked the names of the chapters'

Anya, age 7¾

'All my friends had their heads stuck
in this book!'
Abby, age 7

'I enjoyed reading this book'
Eniolu, age 9

'This book is very exciting'
Joshan, age 8

'It had funny bits and exciting bits.
My favourite part was the end but
I'm not saying what happens!'
Freddie, age 10

EGMONT
We bring stories to life

First published in Great Britain 2010
by Egmont UK Limited
239 Kensington High Street, London W8 6SA

Text and illustrations © 2010 Beckham Brand Ltd
adidas, Predator, the 3-Bars logo and the 3-Stripes are registered
trademarks of the adidas Group, used with permission

Text by Barry Hutchison
Cover and inside illustrations by Adam Relf
Cover photography by Anthony Mandler
Edited by Emily Stead. Designed by Jo Bestall

ISBN 978 1 4052 5164 8

1 3 5 7 9 10 8 6 4 2

A CIP catalogue record for this title is available
from the British Library

Printed and bound in Great Britain by the CPI Group

FSC
Mixed Sources
Product group from well-managed
forests and other controlled sources
Cert no. TT-COC-002332
www.fsc.org
© 1996 Forest Stewardship Council

Egmont is passionate about helping to preserve the world's remaining ancient forests.
We only use paper from legal and sustainable forest sources.

This book is made from paper certified by the Forestry Stewardship Council (FSC),
an organisation dedicated to promoting responsible management of forest resources.
For more information on the FSC, please visit www.fsc.org. To learn more about
Egmont's sustainable paper policy, please visit www.egmont.co.uk/ethical

THE DAVID BECKHAM
ACADEMY

AWAY FROM HOME

EGMONT

CONTENTS

GOING DUTCH

George polished his glasses and put them back on.

'I don't get it. If we're Holland, why don't we get orange kits?'

Ben sighed as he pulled the blue David Beckham Academy football shirt over his head.

'Look, we're not *really* Holland,' he explained for the second time. 'That's just a name for our team. That lot over there are France. And I know they're not French because three of them go to my school!'

'So we aren't going to have a Dutch coach then?' George asked.

'No,' said Ben patiently. 'We'll have an English coach. We're just *called* Holland.'

George seemed to get the message at last and bent down to lace up his football boots. 'Well, I don't see why they have to make it so confusing!' he muttered.

Ben was about to suggest that it was actually quite simple when three more boys shoved their way through the huddle in the boys' changing room.

'Are you lot Holland?' asked a tall boy with scruffy brown hair.

'Yep!' nodded Ben. 'Welcome to the team! I'm Ben and this is George.'

The team members quickly introduced themselves and pulled on their new football kits.

'So who's your favourite player?' asked George, smoothing down his ginger hair in a nearby mirror.

'David Beckham, of course!' said Ben, checking his own crop of curly black hair in the mirror. 'What about you?'

Within minutes, all the members of the Holland team were arguing about their favourite players and boasting about how

they were *definitely* going to be the best team at The Academy.

'I'm telling you guys, we *have* to win!' cried Ben.

'Yeah!' cried George. 'How about we pick our positions before the coach gets here? I play on the left wing!'

'I'm a midfielder,' said Ben.

'I play in midfield too!' said another boy.

'What about you?' said George, to a short boy with dark, spiky hair who had just joined the group. 'What's your favourite position?'

The boy looked blankly at George and didn't answer.

'Hey!' said Ben, assuming the boy hadn't heard. 'You're in Holland, right? What's your name?'

The boy looked blank again and

shrugged nervously.

'You must know your name!' said Ben. 'What are you called?'

The boy's face suddenly lit up. 'Stefan!' he said in a foreign accent.

'Aha!' said George. 'I knew it! A Dutchman!'

Ben rolled his eyes. 'Will you shut up about Dutchmen? I've told you . . .'

But George was questioning Stefan in a slow, loud voice.

'Are . . . you . . . from . . . Holland?' he asked, mouthing the words as he spoke. Stefan just shrugged again.

'Do . . . you . . . speak . . . English?' George continued.

Stefan seemed to understand and shook his head. 'No English,' he said.

George looked smugly at Ben. 'See!' he

said. 'He's not English. He's *definitely* from Holland!'

Ben groaned. 'Just because he's foreign, doesn't mean he's Dutch!' he replied with a sigh. 'He doesn't even have a Dutch accent!'

Stefan seemed to realise they were talking about him and started to blush. He began fidgeting with a pile of football stickers in his shorts pocket.

'So what kind of accent *does* he have, then?' asked George.

Ben hesitated. 'Well, it's obvious, isn't it?' he began, uncertainly, but he didn't add anything more.

Before George could quiz Ben further, Stefan took the stickers from his pocket and began shuffling through them. The other boys gathered round, studying each sticker as it was flicked from the top to the bottom of the pack.

Names flashed by in a blur – Jodlowiec, Komorowski, Boruc – each name as unfamiliar as the one before.

George called out excitedly as a shiny foil sticker caught his eye. 'Hey, that's the Polish flag! It was the very last sticker I swapped to finish my album,' he announced. 'Poland have finished third in two World Cups – 1974 and 1982, you know.'

Ben laughed. 'Someone knows their stats!'

'So Stefan, that means you're from Poland, right?' asked George.

'Polska!' nodded Stefan, feeling encouraged.

'Mystery solved,' smiled Ben. He reached into his own pocket and took out a pile of stickers held together in an elastic band. Holding them out to Stefan, he asked, 'Know any of these guys?'

Stefan frowned and shook his head at the first few footballers in Ben's collection. He knew quite a few of the famous players at British clubs, but the faces on these stickers were as unfamiliar to him as the Polish players had been to the other boys.

'How about this one?' said Ben, stopping

halfway through the pack. He held up the most prized of all his stickers. 'You must have heard of him!'

'BECK-HAM!' smiled Stefan, giving Ben the thumbs-up.

'That's right!' replied Ben, approvingly. 'David Beckham.'

'I'd be surprised if you didn't know who Beckham was,' laughed George. 'We are at his Academy, after all!'

The boys were still comparing stickers when a tallish woman in a smart Academy tracksuit knocked on the changing room door. 'I'm Kelly, your coach for the next few days,' she addressed the team. 'Ready for training, Holland?'

'You bet!' cried George, excitedly. He waited until Kelly had left before whispering to Ben, 'Holland. That's us, right?'

'*Yes!*' laughed Ben, leading the other boys out into the corridor. 'Now let's go get us some goals.'

TEAM TALK

The Holland team were puffing and panting as they finished their warm-up. An area beside the main pitch had been coned off for them to work on their football skills. All around them, the other teams' practice sessions were already in full swing.

Kelly finished laying out the last few coloured cones, then strode over to join the team.

'OK, now that we've all warmed up, we'll start with an easy drill,' she said. 'This one's designed to test your ball control. Stay focused, and you'll be fine.'

Kelly explained exactly what she wanted them to do. The boys all nodded to show that they had understood. All except one.

Stefan frowned. He'd tried to follow what Kelly had been saying, but the coach had been speaking fast. Was he supposed to dribble alongside the row of cones, or through them? He wasn't sure.

Kelly gave Stefan a quick thumbs-up to check he'd understood and Stefan did the same back to her. He didn't want to look stupid in front of the others.

Ben bounced a ball in front of him confidently. He was the captain of his school team – he was used to going first.

Kelly blew the whistle and Ben set off, quickly weaving through the cones. He took lots of little touches and always kept the

ball just in front of him. He rounded the last cone and joined the back of the queue, feeling pleased.

Stefan let out a sigh of relief. After watching Ben, he knew exactly what he had to do. He was relaxed, and set off quickly when Kelly nodded at him to go next.

In fact, Stefan's attempt was even better than Ben's. He dribbled through the cones, using both feet to control the ball. He was easily as good as some of the taller boys, never letting the ball wander from his feet, and he made it through the cones a couple of seconds faster than Ben had.

As he finished, Stefan rolled his foot over the ball, flicked it into the air and caught it. He jogged up behind Ben without so much as a bead of sweat on his lip.

'Not bad!' panted Ben as he caught his breath. 'Not bad at all.'

Stefan smiled uncertainly, not sure what Ben had said to him. When Ben gave him a thumbs up though, Stefan's smile widened, and he held up his own thumb too.

'You were brilliant!' cried George as he joined them. George had fumbled the ball through the cones, but he'd still reached the end in good time. 'Both of you!'

'Thanks,' said Ben, in a matter-of-fact

voice. 'You weren't too bad yourself.'

Ben looked around at the other teams, then turned back to his own. 'You know what?' he smiled. 'I reckon we might just win this thing.'

● ● ●

The skills training passed quickly, and after an energy-boosting lunch of pasta, it was soon time for the afternoon tournament. Kelly nominated Ben to organise the team into their positions. Ben asked where everyone wanted to play.

'I'm always central midfield, if that's all right with everyone?' he began bossily, without waiting for an answer. 'George is left-footed so we'll stick him on the left wing, and I think we could use your height up front,' he said, gesturing to a tall girl with braided hair.

Stefan pretended to tie up his bootlace as Ben turned to him next.

'Stefan, what position do you play? Defence, midfield, lone striker?' Ben asked him.

Ben was talking very quickly and Stefan couldn't remember the words for football positions that his dad had taught him. He muttered something that didn't sound to Ben like any position on the pitch.

'Sorry, my Polish is worse than your English!' Ben joked to Stefan. 'Where do you want to play?'

Stefan chewed his lip, worriedly. He could feel everyone watching him now, waiting for him to answer, but he couldn't find the right words to use. His cheeks stung red with embarrassment. He had to find a way of making them understand.

Giving up on words, Stefan decided to try miming. He ran on the spot, dodging and weaving left to right, then swung hard as if he were kicking an imaginary ball.

'If he keeps that up he'll be exhausted before we've kicked off,' remarked George.

Ben didn't reply. He was staring at Stefan who now had his arms out to the side, miming a goal celebration. But Ben took the gesture to mean something else completely.

'He's pretending to block someone,' Ben said. 'OK then, Stefan, if you're sure that's what you want. You can play in defence.'

● ● ●

Ben and George were standing in the centre circle, ready for their match against Mexico to start. They'd both been surprised that Stefan played in defence, and were worried what it might mean for the team.

'It's funny . . . with his skills, I'd have had him down as a striker every time,' said Ben, running his fingers through his dark, curly hair. 'Shame he'd rather play at the back.'

'We could do with a proper striker,' George agreed.

Behind them, Stefan didn't look happy. Not once had he played in defence for his school team back in Poland. Striker? Sure. Midfield? Sometimes. He'd even been in goal once when the school keeper had had to come off injured. But defence? Never.

The captains shook hands and the match kicked off. Mexico soon had possession of the ball, and began stringing together their passes nicely.

Before long, an olive-skinned boy was quickly bearing down on a nervous Stefan. Stefan swallowed hard. He wasn't much

good at tackling. With the Mexico player
looming large above him, Stefan took a deep
breath, shut his eyes, and lunged . . .

THE CHALLENGE

Stefan braced himself for impact as he waited to make contact with the attacking player. But all he felt was the turf skidding under him, and a sudden *thud* as he landed in a heap.

He opened his eyes and realised his tackle had missed by miles. Behind him, the net shook as the ball rocketed into the Holland goal and Holland went 1–0 down.

'It's OK, Stefan, don't worry about it,' shouted Ben. He was clapping his hands, trying to encourage his teammate, but Stefan could see the disappointment on his face.

Springing back to his feet, Stefan tried to forget about his mistake and focus on the rest of the game. It was only one goal. They could easily come back from that.

George and Ben took the kick-off, and Ben pushed up into the Mexico half, guiding the ball past an oncoming midfielder. As another player raced to stop him, Ben flicked the ball to his left. It bounced once, then landed directly at George's feet.

Stefan's heart raced as he watched the Mexico defence close in on George. Ben was waving his arms, calling for the cross, but there was already a defender goal-side of him – George couldn't pass safely to him. He needed someone on the left.

As if on autopilot, Stefan broke into a run. The ground flew by beneath him as he sprinted up the pitch, desperate to receive the pass. All George would have to do was tap the ball left, and Stefan would have a clear shot at goal. The angle would be tight but –

No!

A tall, skinny boy on the Mexico team took the ball from George and booted it almost the entire length of the pitch. Stefan skidded to a stop, but could only watch the ball sail above his head. He turned back towards the Holland end in time to see the same blond-haired striker chest the ball down, right outside the box.

The other Holland defender was on the other side of the pitch, too far away to make any difference. The Mexico player struck the ball cleanly. The keeper dived for it spectacularly, getting a fingertip to the ball.

But Stefan heard Ben groan as it slipped past the goalkeeper's glove, and Mexico went 2–0 up.

This time there were no encouraging words from Ben. Stefan hurried back to his position, keeping his head low. He should have stayed in defence. He should never have charged forwards like that. It wouldn't happen again.

The whistle blew and this time it was George pushing up towards the Mexico goalmouth. Stefan looked down at his legs. It was as if someone was pressing a remote control – they were moving without Stefan telling them to! He soon found himself up the field alongside George. He knew if he could just get to the ball he could slip it past the keeper.

George crossed to Ben, but a powerful

header from a Mexico defender sent the ball soaring back towards the halfway line. Stefan backpedalled to intercept it, but an opposition midfielder beat him to it. He slid in with a tackle, but missed again.

Before Stefan was even back on his feet, Mexico had scored a third.

'Three–nil, I don't believe it,' George groaned. 'What's Stefan doing?'

'No idea,' Ben snapped, angry at how the game was going. 'Stay in defence,' he told Stefan. He thrust an arm towards the Mexico goal. 'Stop playing so high, OK? Don't keep running up that end.'

Stefan smiled weakly and nodded. He didn't know what Ben was saying, but he could guess from the way he was pointing. Ben wanted him to keep pushing forwards and supporting the strikers. This was more like it!

Happy, Stefan returned to his position. As soon as Ben and George had taken the kick-off, he was racing to join them, already picturing the goal he was sure he would soon score.

'He's doing it again!' cried George. 'He's completely out of position!'

Ben glanced back for just a second, but a second was all the Mexico midfielder needed to nick the ball from him. Startled, Ben stumbled and fell clumsily on the turf.

'Stefan, get back!' he bellowed, watching Mexico race up the field with the ball. 'Stop him, stop him, *stop him*!'

Confused by all the shouting, Stefan was slow to react. He saw the ball arc through the air and raced to catch up with it, but he was already far too late. With a thwack,

Mexico made the scoreline 4–0.

A few minutes later, the final whistle blew, and a disappointed Holland trudged off the pitch.

'I can't believe Stefan . . . running out of defence like that,' Ben seethed. 'He cost us the game.'

George nodded. 'Probably,' he agreed, 'although not having a natural striker up front didn't help matters, either.'

Stefan trailed behind the rest of the team. He couldn't understand their conversation, but he could tell they were angry with him. He didn't blame them. He was angry with himself.

Kelly handed him a bottle of water. Stefan thanked her without looking up. The worst thing was, he knew he could have made a difference if he hadn't been stuck in defence. Well, at least this was only the first of his three days at The Academy. He would have to make sure he got to play up front tomorrow, and show everyone exactly what he could do.

LOST IN TRANSLATION

The next day, Stefan was feeling a bit more cheerful. Training had gone well that morning and lunchtime had come around quickly.

In the canteen, Stefan pointed to a baked potato hungrily, and nodded as a helping of tuna was spooned on to his tray.

'Thank-YOU,' he said, shyly. After helping himself to a drink, Stefan crossed the canteen and sat down with the rest of Team Holland at one of the long tables.

Ben and George had plumped for the

Spaghetti Bolognese and were making a real mess trying to eat it — there was pasta and sauce all over the table.

'Watch this,' said Ben, slurping up a string of spaghetti at super-speed. Tomato sauce dribbled down his chin.

'Gross!' said a girl sitting across from them, another defender in the Dutch team.

George spluttered with laughter, spraying juice in all directions. But when Stefan joined in, Ben and the rest of the Holland team just stared at him, coolly.

'I don't know why he's laughing after his performance yesterday,' said Ben harshly. 'We've got to sort ourselves out at the back if we're going to stand a chance of getting through the next round.'

'Well, I didn't exactly get much protection,' moaned Robbie, the sandy-haired keeper. He hadn't had a good game either, and was looking to shift the blame on to someone else. He turned to Stefan. 'You've got to stick to your player like glue!' he explained.

'Gloo?' repeated Stefan, turning red. He had no idea what the word meant, but there was something he could do about that.

Watched by the rest of the team, Stefan pulled out a small device from his pocket.

'Is that a calculator?' asked one boy.

'Oh, great,' scowled Ben, 'he thinks we'll need a calculator to figure out how much we're losing by.'

The device did look a bit like a calculator, but it had letters where the numbers should have been. The night before, Stefan had had a brainwave, and had packed his dad's handheld electronic translator in his kitbag.

I've got to make them understand that I'm a striker, not a defender. I should be playing up front, thought Stefan. He typed on the keypad and held the screen close to his face. 'I ATTACK!' he exclaimed loudly.

The players closest to Stefan leaned backwards, suddenly nervous.

'Now hang on a minute,' Ben began, 'there's no need to start acting all tough —'

Stefan cut him short. 'I STRIKE!' he beamed, flashing the translator under Ben's nose.

Ben went scarlet. 'What did you say?' he yelled, angrily. 'Are you going to try to hit me?'

Kelly overheard the boys arguing, and quickly hurried over to the table. 'What's all the noise about?' she asked, firmly.

'Stefan said he's going to beat Ben up,' said George, taking off his glasses to polish them on his shirt.

Kelly turned to Stefan. 'Is this true?' she asked.

'I attack,' Stefan said again.

Kelly frowned. 'I don't think Stefan's trying to cause trouble,' she told the team. 'Look, he's smiling! Stefan's still learning English, so I want us all to try to help him out. I can't quite work out what he means, but I really don't think it's anything sinister.'

Ben stood up, and the rest of the team —all except Stefan—did the same. 'Whatever,' Ben shrugged. 'Come on, guys. Let's go out there and take another beating.'

'What kind of attitude is that?' asked Kelly, folding her arms. 'OK, so you had a minor setback yesterday, but it's a whole new day today. Let's see a positive mental attitude out there. Let your feet do the talking, OK?'

'Fine,' sighed Ben, but it was clear he was feeling far from positive. He and his teammates cleared their trays and trudged out of the canteen, shaking their heads. First Stefan had made them lose their opening game, and now he was shouting about attacking them in the canteen. Their patience with him was running thin.

As the team filed along the corridor, Ben turned to George. 'Positive mental attitude or not, there's no way we're going to win,' he huffed. 'We've got no proper strikers and our defence lets in more goals than San Marino.'

'Maybe we'll get lucky,' George suggested.

Ben glanced back at Stefan, who had joined the line. 'The way Stefan's been playing, it's not luck we need,' he muttered. 'It's a miracle.'

Stefan slunk along at the back of the queue, feeling miserable and alone. *Why is everyone being so mean? All I want to do is play football*, he thought to himself.

He was still lost in his thoughts as they

strode out on to the pitch. Ben pulled him to one side, snapping Stefan out of his daydream.

'Right, we'll give you another go in defence, and this time try not to mess up, will you?' said Ben bossily. He pointed to the same defensive area Stefan had started in yesterday.

Great, thought Stefan. They still don't

understand me and now I have to play in defence again.

A few minutes later as the game kicked off, Stefan was daydreaming again. In Poland, he went to a small school in the village where he'd lived all his life. The school team had grown up together, and Stefan, being one of the best players, always got to play up front. He sighed, wishing he were back there now. His old teammates appreciated him, and his goals.

He'd thought coming to England would be fun, but playing for a brand new team was harder than he'd thought.

FROM BAD TO WORSE

Things started well for Holland in their game against Spain. Straight from the kick-off, Ben mounted an attack, weaving expertly past the Spanish defence. His powerful shot at goal went a little too high, though, clipping the top of the crossbar and going out for a goal kick.

'Good effort,' said another Holland player, encouragingly.

'Cheers,' smiled Ben running back into a defensive position.

WHUMPH! Team Spain's goalkeeper was

a strong, stocky boy, and with one kick he lofted the ball three-quarters of the way up the pitch. Stefan was already chasing back, determined that this time he wouldn't let the team – or himself – down.

But before Stefan could get there, Ben sprinted for the same ball. He trapped it beneath his right foot, then spun on the spot so his back was facing the oncoming Stefan. With a grunt, Ben chipped the ball over a defender and back up into the Spain half, where George collected it.

Stefan stopped, amazed that Ben had stolen the ball from him.

Fine, thought Stefan, *if they don't trust me to defend, I'll attack instead.*

Powering forwards, Stefan began to catch up with Ben. The two boys were soon running side by side, much to Ben's horror.

'What are you doing?' he demanded. 'Get back down the other end.'

Suddenly, George cried, 'One of you!'

Ben and Stefan saw a flash of leather pass above their heads, and realised George had lost the ball. They both stopped, turned and began to run back towards their own goal.

A Holland midfielder sprung high for the ball, throwing himself towards it, head-first. His jump fell short though, and the ball bounced past him, straight to the waiting feet of a dark-haired girl wearing the colours of Team Spain.

'No, no, no! Not again!' Ben roared, as some fancy footwork from the girl nudged Spain into the lead.

He glared at Stefan, too angry to even speak. Stefan tried a friendly smile, even though he knew Ben wouldn't smile back.

Feeling miserable, and wishing more than ever that he was back home in Poland, Stefan made the long, lonely walk back to defence.

Upset at losing such a stupid goal, Team Holland lost what little fighting spirit they had left. By the end of a terrible first half, they were 4–0 down *again*, and Ben knew exactly who was to blame.

'I swear, my granny would make a better defender,' he groaned as both teams stopped for a drink and to discuss tactics. 'And my granny only has one leg!'

'He's not that bad,' said George, weakly.

Ben sighed. 'OK, Stefan,' he said, 'I'm going to give you one more chance, but you've got to stay in position, OK? Stay in position, understand? Understand?'

'Un-der-STAND,' repeated Stefan. This word he knew, at least.

The kick-off was clumsy, and for a few moments the ball just seemed to bounce randomly between players on both teams. Finally, a boy from Team Spain found himself with the ball at his feet. He made a frantic run up the field, with Ben bearing down on him.

Panicking, the boy kicked the ball as hard

as he could. He was still a long way from the goal though, and the ball had slowed to a roll by the time it came towards Stefan.

'Clear it up the field,' called the Holland keeper, who was kneeling by the left post, tying a shoelace that had come loose.

Misunderstanding the instruction, Stefan lifted his foot, let the ball roll under it, then knocked his heel against it, sending it back towards where he thought the goalkeeper was waiting to kick it out.

'What are you doing?' cried the keeper. The panic in his voice made Stefan spin around, just as the ball rolled across the line and into the Holland goal.

'That's it. You're off!' fumed Ben, scowling at Stefan and calling for a substitute to come on.

Stefan turned on his heel and stormed

off the pitch. He felt tears prick his eyes, but managed to hold them back. *I won't cry, I won't cry*, he told himself.

He slammed through the swing doors and found himself in the Hall of Fame. Wandering into the dimly lit room, he stopped to look at the famous trophies, and framed shirts worn by football's greatest players from all over the world.

Staring at a pristine white Real Madrid shirt, with David Beckham's signature scrawled on it, Stefan's expression began to change. *When Beckham signed for Real Madrid, he didn't know how to speak Spanish, did he? And his teammates probably didn't speak much English either*, Stefan wondered. *It can't have been easy.*

He allowed himself the smallest of smiles. Now he just had to work out a way to make Ben and the others understand him. He turned around, stopping for a second by the doorway to the classroom.

In the classroom one of the coaches, Woody, was setting up a tactics board ready for a lesson with another group at The Academy. He smiled at Stefan, 'You lost, son?'

As Woody bent down to pick up

a magnet, Stefan stared at the board. *That's it!* thought Stefan. *That's really it!* He sprinted off to the pitches without saying a word.

'Hello?' Woody called after him.

But Stefan had disappeared.

A CHANGE OF TACTICS

The final whistle had just blown as Stefan stepped on to the turf. The Holland team looked miserable, and no wonder – they had been thrashed 5–2. They would have to win all their remaining games if they were going to win the tournament and had only qualified for the next round on goal difference – by a single goal.

'We were useless out there,' said Ben, turning to George. 'I mean, you and me were OK, and some of the others played well enough, but we're rubbish at the back.'

'We didn't exactly shine up front, either,' George pointed out. 'Whenever I had the ball, there was no one to cross to in the box – the forwards were playing too deep, trying to help tackle back,' he grumbled.

Ben looked down at his laces. Yesterday, he'd believed his team could win the tournament. Now they'd be lucky to avoid coming in last place. If only Stefan had performed on the pitch as well as he had done in training, they might have stood a chance.

'Hey!' he scowled, when a hand caught him by the sleeve and tugged hard. He turned to find Stefan standing beside him, grinning. 'What do you want, Stefan?' Ben asked with a sigh. 'If you're going to complain about the final score, don't bother. We could have lost ten–two if I hadn't subbed you.'

Stefan let go of Ben's arm, but kept smiling. He hadn't understood a single word that Ben had said, but that no longer mattered. He didn't need words to explain himself now.

'What's he doing?' asked George, when Stefan began beckoning them towards the door that led into the main building.

'I'm not sure,' frowned Ben. 'I think he wants us to go with him.'

For a moment, no one moved. But then George shrugged and began walking after Stefan. 'Might as well,' he said, 'it can't exactly hurt at this stage, can it?'

One by one, the rest of the team followed, until only Ben was left behind. He watched them make their way through the swing doors.

'Fine,' he muttered, rolling his eyes, 'let's see what he's got to say.'

Stefan sped back towards the classroom excitedly, with the rest of the team trailing behind. His plan was working, and he felt a sudden rush of happiness. Maybe everything was going to work out OK, after all!

Arriving well ahead of the rest of the team, Stefan tapped his foot impatiently, waiting for the others to join him. When they finally trudged through the door, he smiled broadly and gestured for them to gather round.

Ben remained by the door, his arms folded across his chest. Part of him felt bad for being so mean to Stefan, but what else could he have done? It was Stefan's fault they

had lost their first two games. Stefan was the one who'd asked to play in defence, and then he'd spent both games trying to play in nearly every position except defence. No wonder they kept losing.

George and the other Holland players gathered together at the front of the classroom as Stefan began to arrange coloured magnets on the whiteboard. At the bottom of the board he stuck four magnets in a row. Above that row, he added another five magnets, spaced out, but still pretty much straight. And then, above this row, he stuck just one final magnet, right in the middle of the board.

'That's . . . smart,' said George, kindly. 'What is it?'

'It's a 4–5–1 formation,' Ben explained, stepping into the room. 'Four defenders, five in midfield, and a lone striker up front.'

'Of course,' said George, nodding quickly. 'I knew that.'

Stefan wasn't paying them any attention. He picked up the magnet from the very centre of the formation and held it up for the others to see.

'Ben,' he said, firmly. He stuck the magnet back in place and pointed to another magnet directly to the left. 'George,' said Stefan.

Stefan's plan was going well. People began to nod, slowly. This time, he pointed to the magnet in front of the midfield ones. The one that was way up front on its own. 'I attack!' smiled Stefan.

'Oh! You mean you're an *attacker* — a striker! I can't believe we've been so dumb!' laughed George, pressing his hand to his forehead.

Ben said nothing.

Watched by the team, Stefan began drawing lines on the board, each line representing a pass of the ball. George was impressed by the tactics Stefan was suggesting. No words were spoken, but everyone understood Stefan perfectly.

'This could work,' George said, nodding thoughtfully. 'If Stefan can keep control of the ball, this could actually work.'

'That's a big *if*,' Ben replied. 'We've all seen how he's been playing, what makes you think he can pull off any of the stuff he's drawn on there?'

The other members of Team Holland began muttering among themselves. Ben had a point. Stefan hadn't had a sniff of a goal so far, so why should they listen to him now?

'I say we give him a chance,' said George, pushing his glasses further up his nose. 'The worst that can happen is that we lose, and let's face it, we're doing a pretty good job of that already. We might as well try Stefan's tactics.' He glanced across to Ben, who had folded his arms again. 'What do you say, Ben?'

Ben hesitated, suddenly feeling every eye in the room on him. He looked at the board, then across to Stefan. Slowly, Ben nodded his head.

'OK,' he said, 'let's do it!'

THE COMEBACK KINGS

'You sure about this, Ben?' asked the Holland goalkeeper as they returned to the pitch.

Ben shrugged. 'No matter how bad he is up front, it can't be any worse than his defending,' he said. 'Maybe he'll surprise us.'

'Let's hope you're right.'

With that, the Holland team made their way on to the pitch, ready for their game against Brazil. In the pre-match team talk, Kelly had told them that Brazil were a good team, but that if Holland concentrated and had confidence it should be an even match.

They had no choice — Holland had to somehow scrape a win if they were to avoid being knocked out of the tournament.

As soon as the whistle blew to start the game, Brazil were off. They took the kick-off quickly, launching into a quick one–two that beat two of Holland's defenders.

Ben thundered towards the ball, forcing the Brazil player to pass it low along the ground to his teammate. With a burst of speed, George cut out the pass, and dribbled up the pitch, back into Brazil's half.

'Remember the magnets!' Ben cried, sidestepping his marker and sprinting after his friend. George thought back to the classroom and hurriedly replayed Stefan's tactics in his head. He remembered the lines Stefan had drawn on the board, and he suddenly realised exactly what he should do.

With a swing of his left leg, George faked to shoot. In the corner of his eye he saw a defender rushing in to put himself in the path of the ball. The Brazil player was tall and broad, and would easily block George's shot.

But George had no intention of shooting. The move had been designed to make the defender commit to the challenge, and it had worked!

Instead of shooting, George chipped the ball across to Ben, who was making a run up the centre of the pitch. With his first touch, Ben knocked the ball on ahead of him, directly towards where Stefan was standing facing his own goal.

As the ball came down, Stefan threw himself backwards. His right knee swung up towards the sky, before his leg straightened,

bringing his boot into contact with the ball.

THWACK! The overhead kick was perfect. The ball rocketed backwards over Stefan's head, curled past the Brazil goalkeeper, and found the top corner of the net.

Back in midfield, Ben and George looked at each other and smiled. 'Now that,' panted Ben, 'is what I call a goal!'

'That was *amazing*,' George laughed, punching the air in delight.

'But let's not get too excited,' warned Ben. 'There's still a long way to go.'

George nodded, but he was finding it difficult to stay calm. Stefan had just pulled off the most incredible goal George had ever seen, and George had a feeling there may well be more where that came from.

George wasn't wrong. When Stefan was in full flow up front, none of the Brazil defenders could touch him. He twisted around midfielders. He flicked the ball over defenders' heads. Before long, he'd hammered home a hat-trick, each goal more brilliant than the one before.

And it wasn't just Stefan who was playing well. Re-energised by Stefan's incredible performance, the rest of the team had also upped their game. They were working well together, and by the end of the first half, they had really found their rhythm. Now, with only five minutes left to go, they were playing like champions.

It was a tired and miserable Brazil that took the last kick-off of the game. Ben raced for the ball, taking it easily from the Brazil player's exhausted feet. With a quick look up, Ben sent the ball sailing out to the wing, where it was collected by George.

A silky step-over and George had beaten his marker. He squared a pass to Stefan, who received the ball with his back to goal. The defender was right on top of him . . . there was nowhere to go. But Stefan tried a cheeky backheel and slipped the ball through the defender's legs into the path of Ben, who had charged forwards from midfield. With the inside of his foot, Ben cushioned the ball low into the corner of the net, away from the keeper.

'Gooooal!' screamed the Holland players together.

'That's the easiest goal I'm ever going to score!' laughed Ben.

The whole team was still singing 'Four–nil, four–nil, four–nil, four–nil!' long after the final whistle had blown.

● ● ●

In the changing rooms, Ben turned to Stefan, looking sheepish. 'Listen, I'm sorry I was a bit hard on you before, mate,' he began. 'I just wanted us to win the tournament so badly.'

Stefan wasn't sure what Ben was saying, but he could guess the meaning.

He bent down to pat Ben's right boot. 'David Beckham!' he beamed.

'I think that's his way of saying you're a decent midfielder,' George said, and Ben smiled gratefully.

'Can I use this?' Ben asked, spotting the translator poking out of Stefan's kitbag.

He pushed a few buttons, frowned, then said firmly, 'VEEL-KEE STRY-KOO-JON-KEE.'

Stefan laughed and clapped his hands, then took the translator back and began typing a message of his own.

'It means "great striker",' Ben explained to George.

It was Stefan's turn to study the device's small screen. His lips moved silently as he tried out the words. When he was sure he had them correct, he turned to the rest of the team.

'We . . . must . . . win.'

Ben gave Stefan a friendly pat on the back. 'Couldn't have put it better myself.'

WORLD CLASS

George could feel his heart thumping like a car stereo. It was the final ten minutes of the final game. These were the last few touches he would have of the ball here at The Academy, and he was determined to make the most of them.

Yesterday had been an amazing day, with Stefan's tactics helping keep alive Holland's dream of winning the tournament. The morning training session had been brilliant, with everyone laughing and joking together. Lunch had been much more of a team event too. George and Ben had spent the break teaching Stefan some English words, and Stefan had taught them how to say a few things in Polish in return.

But right now, George wasn't thinking about any of that. He was wrapped up in the game, devastated that Germany had just scored.

'We're still two–one up,' Ben reminded his team as George set the ball down on the centre spot. 'It's not long until the final whistle. We can do this, right?'

'Right,' nodded George.

The whistle blew. Ben tapped the ball gently and ran forwards, ready to receive a short pass back from George.

'Good . . . ball, George!' shouted Stefan. He still spoke quite slowly, but his English was getting better.

A German player slid towards Ben, his foot outstretched. Ben sprayed a pass out to another of the Holland midfielders, who pressed on up the wing.

'Stefan, get into space,' Ben shouted.

Stefan hesitated, trying to work out what Ben had said. All he could think of was the book about stars and planets his dad had bought him. Finally, he looked up at the roof, and Ben couldn't help but laugh.

'Not that kind of space!' Ben called, pointing to an area by the far post that was completely unmarked. 'That kind of space.'

Stefan grinned sheepishly, then sprinted up the field. 'Here!' he cried, waving his arm to indicate he was free.

The Holland player stopped and swung a cross into the box. Two German defenders were on the alert and went thundering towards the ball.

But Stefan was determined to get there before them. He leapt high into the air and met the ball with a towering header. It bounced hard into the ground and up over the keeper on the floor, crossing the line just as the final whistle blew.

Team Holland went wild! They ran at Stefan and scooped him up on to their

shoulders. Stefan smiled when they began chanting his name, then laughed as they tried some of the Polish words they had learned from his translator. '*Champion*'. '*Hero*'. Stefan blushed with pride.

● ● ●

'I'm so proud of you all,' beamed Kelly as she led the team to where they would be collecting their medals. Despite their terrible start, they had come back to win the tournament, and they had done it as a team.

'Who gives out the medals?' asked George.

'Funny you should ask,' said Kelly, with a smile.

Ben and the rest of the team stopped dead. There, standing just a few metres in front of them, was the man himself . . .

'David Beckham . . . in the flesh!' Ben whispered.

'No way!' George grinned.

Stefan's eyes were wide with amazement. 'David Beckham,' he said.

David smiled at the three boys, who were frozen to the spot.

'Well, up you go then, captain,' said Kelly, giving Ben a nudge. 'Collect the trophy.'

'No,' said Ben, suddenly. The others stared at him, shocked. 'Not without Stefan,' he continued. 'Without him, we'd have finished last. He should be up there, not me.'

Stefan stepped forwards and rested a hand on Ben's shoulder. 'We . . . two . . . go,' he said.

'Excellent suggestion,' agreed George.

'Both of you go up.'

And so it was decided. Side by side, Ben and Stefan stepped forwards, next to the man they had seen hundreds of times on television, the man whose goals they had tried to recreate in their own matches. They each shook his hand in turn, and David Beckham presented them with their own silver medal to take home, and a shiny silver cup.

'Congratulations, guys. I hear your team managed to play together even though you don't all speak the same language,' said David. 'Well done. I know just how hard that can be. When I first moved to Real Madrid I could barely speak a word of Spanish!'

'DYEN-KOO-YE,' Ben said, trying to remember what Stefan had taught him.

'Thank you,' Stefan translated, and the boys exchanged a friendly high five.

'Team photo,' cried Kelly, ushering everyone back on to the pitch. Stefan and Ben took the trophy from David and carried it over to where the rest of the team were already gathered together.

'Hey, Stefan, is that your dad?' asked George, pointing over to where a spiky-haired man with a broad, proud smile was watching them. 'He looks just like you.'

Stefan ran over and hugged his father. Ben and George watched as Stefan's dad leaned and spoke into his son's ear. When Stefan ran back over, he was bouncing excitedly.

'Everything OK, Stefan?' asked George.

'Yes,' Stefan nodded. There was a pause as he tried to remember the words his dad had said. 'I . . . am to be living in Lon-don,' he said, slowly.

And Ben and Stefan were even more excited when they found out that Stefan would be starting at Ben's school after the holidays.

'Awesome!' Ben cried, already thinking what a great addition his new friend would be to the school team.

And everyone was delighted when

David Beckham jogged over to join them for the team photo. They didn't need to be told to smile for this photograph. Every member of the team was grinning from ear to ear!

'Here's to England and Poland,' Ben said as the camera flashed.

'And Wales,' added George.

'Wales?'

'Well, my grandad's Welsh, so that makes me half Welsh. I could play for Wales or England when I grow up!'

'So,' said Ben, resisting the urge to laugh, 'you're Welsh, he's Polish, we're English and we're all playing for Holland. You were right the other day,' he nodded, 'it is confusing!'

As the laughter of his new friends echoed around him, Stefan gave a happy sigh. England was starting to feel like home already.

But Stefan would always support Poland in the World Cup!

TURN THE PAGE TO READ
A SNEAK PREVIEW OF

 CAPTAIN INCREDIBLE

THE SIXTH BOOK IN
THE DAVID BECKHAM ACADEMY
SERIES!

THE ROAD TO THE ACADEMY

Dan Williams sat in the tube-train seat, his hands gripped to the armrests, as the train hurtled through a pitch-black tunnel. Although he knew it wouldn't get them there any quicker, Dan kept his eyes tight shut, willing the train to go faster.

In the seat next to him, his aunt Jess was flicking through the pages of a free newspaper. She had offered it to Dan first, but he couldn't concentrate long enough even to read the football reports at the back. Aunt Jess, he saw, was giving the gossip pages her full attention.

The train whirred to a stop and the doors slid open.

'Please remember to take all personal belongings with you as you leave the train,' came the announcement in a sing-song voice.

'One more stop, one more stop,' said Dan under his breath. His stomach growled with nerves.

It was his first time on the London Underground, and Dan didn't like it one bit. The dark tunnels, the people almost standing on your toes . . . *It'll be worth it when we get there,* thought Dan.

In the carriage behind, Veejay Ganesh – or VJ as he was known to his friends – and his grandpa were heading for the same destination.

VJ's eyes scanned the tube map across

from him. *Were they nearly there?*

Then came a nudge from Grandpa
Ganesh, 'Next stop for The David Beckham
Academy!' the old man winked.

VJ sprang up from his seat and stood by
the door, ready to jump out the very second
the train stopped at the platform.

He had been looking forward to this for
months. Football was all VJ thought about,

from the moment he opened his eyes to the gallery of posters plastered on his bedroom wall in the morning, to when his mum or dad were calling him in at night after hours of keepy-ups practice.

'That football's like your best friend,' his dad would joke. 'You're never apart.'

His 'best friend' sometimes got him into trouble, though. The pair weren't too popular with the neighbours, whose garage doors VJ used for shooting practice.

At school too, VJ would stare out of the window at the football pitches for hours, imagining scoring the goal that would take England to the World Cup and being congratulated by David Beckham and Steven Gerrard.

THWACK! VJ would jerk awake only to find his teacher rapping his textbook on the desk in front of him. Extra maths homework. *Again.*

His grandpa was his biggest fan and never missed any of VJ's matches, not even the friendlies. If the school team were suddenly to announce they were selling season tickets, his grandpa would be first in the queue to buy one.

Even so, Grandpa Ganesh couldn't help teasing his grandson: 'Football's all very well,' he would say, 'but cricket, now there's a *real* sport.'

All that standing around? Rain stopping play? Cricket wasn't for VJ.

The train lurched into the next station and finally stopped. The four passengers got off and soon found themselves being jostled along with the crowd towards the exit.

Dan stared as panels of stainless steel and

lights glimmered all around him. He'd known that London would be different to the small village where he lived on his family's farm, but this was nothing like he could have imagined. He felt as though he had been blasted into the future, and was now on board a space station in the year 2075.

His daydream was suddenly interrupted.

'Come on, Grandpa!' It was VJ. He was walking so fast, he had almost broken into a jog. He bounded up the escalator steps two at a time, overtaking Dan and Aunt Jess.

It had taken VJ months to persuade his parents to let him come to The Academy, and he was going to make sure he soaked up every second of his two days there.

'Hang on, these old bones can only go so fast,' Grandpa called with a smile.

VJ turned around to reply, but as he did so, he stumbled and knocked his left ankle on the hard metal step. The handrail broke his fall.

'Careful, VJ,' said his Grandpa, trying to calm his grandson down. 'Let's try to get you there in one piece, shall we?'

'I'm fine, stop fussing,' snapped VJ. He shook out his foot in a bid to stop it hurting. *Ouch.*

From a few steps below, Dan watched the scene. VJ was smaller and slimmer than Dan, and kept his dark hair short and spiky. *That boy must be going to The Academy too,* Dan thought, *I wonder if he's any good.*

As the escalator took them back to ground level, Dan breathed a deep sigh. *Daylight!*

The ticket barriers opened, and the boys,

Grandpa and Aunt Jess left the station. They crossed the road to be greeted by the huge arches of The Academy.

'Blimey! This place is massive!' gasped VJ. 'Look at it, Grandpa!'

Dan's jaw hung wide open. He felt his heart begin to beat faster in his chest and the hairs on the back of his neck stand on end. It was so big, you could have fitted the whole of the Williams family's farm in it. Welcome to The David Beckham Academy.

TO BE CONTINUED

Collect all the books in
The David Beckham Academy range

STORY BOOKS

1. Twin Trouble   ISBN 978 1 4052 4524 1   £4.99

2. Le Football   ISBN 978 1 4052 4525 8   £4.99

3. Save the Day   ISBN 978 1 4052 4526 5   £4.99

4. Bossy Boots   ISBN 978 1 4052 4527 2   £4.99

5. Away From Home   ISBN 978 1 4052 5164 8   £4.99

6. Captain Incredible   ISBN 978 1 4052 5165 5   £4.99

ACTIVITY BOOKS

How-to Handbook   ISBN 978 1 4052 4669 9   £4.99

Ultimate Football   ISBN 978 1 4052 4670 5   £4.99
Sticker Book

Champion Cards   ISBN 978 1 4052 5121 1   £4.99
Activity Book

WIN! SIGNED DAVID BECKHAM ACADEMY BOOKS

We're giving away 25 copies of the action-packed footy story **Twin Trouble**, signed by David Beckham himself.*

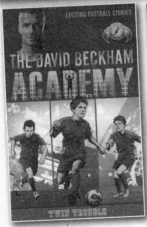

PLUS! More books to collect...

Simply visit
www.egmont.co.uk/academy

*Terms and conditions apply. See online for full details.

E0601